Calf Roping

Kimberly King

The Rosen Publishing Group, Inc., New York

Published in 2006 by The Rosen Publishing Group, Inc.
29 East 21st Street, New York, NY 10010

Copyright © 2006 by The Rosen Publishing Group, Inc.

First Edition

Library of Congress Cataloging-in-Publication Data

King, Kimberly.
Calf roping/Kimberly King.
    p. cm.—(The world of rodeo)
Includes bibliographical references and index.
ISBN 1-4042-0545-4 (library binding)
1. Calf roping—Juvenile literature. I. Title. II. Series.

GV1834.45.C34K56 2006
791.8'4—dc22

2005016468

Manufactured in Malaysia

Cover photo: A cowboy ropes a calf in the Arthur County Rodeo in Arthur County, Nebraska, 1990.

Contents

Introduction   4

Chapter 1   The History of Rodeo   6

Chapter 2   Calf Roping in Action   13

Chapter 3   Great Calf Ropers of the World   20

Chapter 4   Getting Started in Calf Roping   28

List of Champions   36

Glossary   40

For More Information   42

For Further Reading   44

Bibliography   45

Index   47

Introduction

You have been waiting for this moment. Your heart is pounding, but you have practiced this run so much that you have started to dream of it. You back your horse into the farthest corner of the box. You can see the barrier rope over the opening, and you have a view of the calf in the chute. You wait for the signal. The gate opens, and your instinct takes over. Your horse runs behind the calf, you've got one rope in your mouth, and you are swinging the other in a smooth motion. You are about five feet behind the calf, and you know you have a good shot. You throw the rope toward the calf. You see that the rope has a good curl and pull it to tighten the slack. You pull your reins to get your horse to come to a complete stop, expecting the jerk as you dismount him. Your hand follows the rope from the horse to the calf. You block the calf off from running and position yourself over him to get a good grip of his underbelly. You grab hold of the top front leg and begin stringing it as you lift the calf off the ground and onto his side. You then grab the two hind legs and tie the three together, low to the ground. Once this is complete, you throw your hands in the air and wait for your score. Welcome to the sport of calf roping!

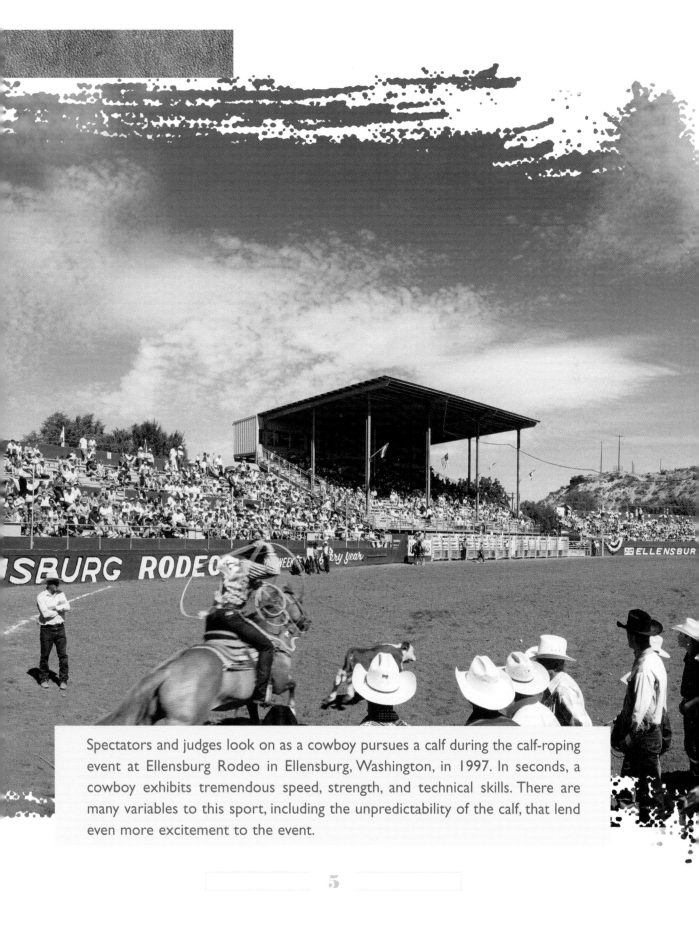

Spectators and judges look on as a cowboy pursues a calf during the calf-roping event at Ellensburg Rodeo in Ellensburg, Washington, in 1997. In seconds, a cowboy exhibits tremendous speed, strength, and technical skills. There are many variables to this sport, including the unpredictability of the calf, that lend even more excitement to the event.

THE HISTORY OF RODEO

CHAPTER 1

Calf roping, also known as tie-down roping, is one of the oldest sports in rodeo. It started in the Old West when sick calves needed to be captured and given medical attention. It is now one of the most competitive events in rodeo. Not only does a roper race against the clock, he or she races against the other ropers competing in the event. It is a sport that requires strength, speed, timing, and technique. Young cowboys and cowgirls are often drawn to the sport of calf roping and other sports of rodeo because they are events built on honor, friendships, and a tradition that started long ago in the Old West.

THE BEGINNING OF RODEO IN THE OLD WEST

Until the early 1800s, Spain possessed most of the land that would become the Western United States. There, missions were established to raise cattle for the thriving American market. The men running these missions came from a long line of Spanish nobility, the conquistadores, who possessed great skills in horsemanship. These horsemen passed along their skills to their workers, or vaqueros, who helped them manage the cattle. When the United States took possession of this land in 1848, more Americans began to enter this market and work right alongside the vaqueros. At least once a year, the cowhands would need to round up the cattle on the open range and move them to various markets. This task was known as a cattle drive. Men who knew how to rope a calf were greatly needed, as the

The ability to rope a calf was a crucial skill for vaqueros (buckaroos) to possess. This 1908 photograph shows two buckaroos in action on a ranch in Texas. Having just captured a calf, a buckaroo heads toward the calf to brand it for identification. As there were no fences in the Old West, branding was necessary.

cattle had to be individually branded with the owner's name or doctored if they got hurt. These skilled men adopted the name "cowboys." During these drives, cowboys would gather together and have contests. They enjoyed showing off their horsemanship and roping ability. It took real talent to hold on to a mustang. The mustang—a direct descendant of the first horses to be brought to North America by the Spanish conquistadores—was the horse of the western plain, often used to round up the cattle. Many mustangs were wild, and some of these cowboys had a real talent for staying in the saddle no matter how hard the mustang bucked. The talent these cowboys had was indeed entertaining. Spectators began to gather, and so began the rodeo.

The World's First Rodeo?

Rodeos began springing up all over North America during the late nineteenth century, making the time and location of the first rodeo hard to determine. A town called Deer Trail, Colorado, claims to have held the first rodeo when two rival groups competed in bronc riding and steer roping on July 4, 1869. The town of Pecos, Texas, also claims to be the home of the world's first rodeo, held on July 4, 1883. Known as West of the Pecos, this rodeo still thrives today.

The term "rodeo" originated from the Spanish word *rodear*, which means "to surround." People started paying to attend cowboy competitions in the 1880s. Over time, the contests began to include judges and rules.

WILD WEST SHOWS

Once the railroad began to connect the eastern United States with the "New West," contestants could travel to various competitions, and spectators could attend shows farther away. One of the most famous shows was Buffalo Bill's Wild West. William F. Cody, born in Scott County, Iowa, in 1846, had earned his nickname, Buffalo Bill, because he provided buffalo meat for the construction crews of the Kansas Pacific Railroad. Cody had been an expert rider for the Pony Express and also worked as a scout for the U.S. Army. He organized his first outdoor Wild West show in 1883. It included reenactments of buffalo hunts, stagecoach robberies, and Indian attacks and war dances. His shows also included cowboys showcasing their ranching skills in various contests. Cody traveled with his troupe all over the United States and even performed in Europe.

Cody had a great eye for talent. In 1885, he discovered sharpshooter Annie Oakley. Oakley could shoot a dime in the air and shoot an apple off a poodle's head. She traveled with Buffalo Bill's troupe for seventeen years.

Bill Pickett, one of the first famous black cowboys, was also discovered by Cody. He is credited with inventing steer wrestling. Pickett could stop the strongest steers with a trick he claimed to have learned from watching bulldogs fight. He would grab a steer by its horns and bite down on its lip with his teeth. This large animal would then stop right in its tracks! The technique became known as "bulldogging." Pickett was one of the first cowboys to perform this event in front of an audience.

A 1922 movie poster advertises Bill Pickett starring in *The Bull-Dogger*. Pickett was of Native American and African descent. He died in 1932 after suffering injuries from being kicked in the head by a horse.

THE BEGINNING OF RODEO ASSOCIATIONS

While the Wild West shows dazzled big city audiences, more "official" rodeo competitions were taking place in cow towns. This trend held until two major events happened: Buffalo Bill's death in 1916, and the U.S. entry into World War I in 1917. The rodeo competitions that had been so popular in the rural areas of the United States then began to move to larger arenas.

In 1929, the promoters, managers, and other producers responsible for staging rodeos created the first rodeo organization, called the Rodeo Association of America (RAA). The RAA created specific rules and regulations for the different events and developed the world champion title. This title went to the contestant who had won the most money by the end of the season, the criterion that still determines the world champion today.

In 1936, a champion calf-roper named Everett Bowman led contestants in a strike out of Boston Garden after the contestants began to get tired of the unfair prize money. This led to the founding of the Cowboy Turtles Association. This name reflected the fact that the organization had been slow to form and fight against the RAA. These cowboys felt exploited because they were not being paid fair wages. They also felt the contests did not have honest judges. In 1945, the association changed its name to Rodeo Cowboys Association and later to Professional Rodeo Cowboys Association (PRCA) in 1975. Today, this organization is the largest in the country, with 700 sanctioned rodeos and $36 million awarded every year. Today the PRCA's Wrangler ProRodeo Tours make it possible for the professional rodeo cowboy to travel less and make a decent living. He can also compete in fewer rodeos and still earn a placement in the finals.

WOMEN IN RODEO

Women have competed in rodeo since the time of Cody's Wild West. Cow town rodeo organizers recognized that women were as strong and fast as men. In the 1920s, Mabel Strickland competed at the Pendleton Round-Up in Oregon. She roped and tied a steer in eighteen seconds. Few men in that era could beat her time. Although they sometimes competed in the same events, women were hardly ever awarded the same kind of prize money as men. They would win prizes such as makeup, luggage, or cigarette cases rather than cash. Most often, rodeos only offered women exhibition events. Otherwise, women would pay entry fees for a Girl's Bronc Riding event and win a cash prize in that event.

The Girl's Professional Rodeo Association (GPRA) was organized in 1948 by a group of ranch women who decided to start their own rodeos. Today, this organization is known as the Women's Professional Rodeo Association (WPRA) and has more than 2,000 members. The WPRA sanctions barrel racing only, while its

Mabel Strickland is pictured here on her horse Stranger in 1924. Strickland was born in Walla Walla, Washington, in 1897. Her father was a bootmaker and introduced her to the rodeo when she was very young. By her teenage years, she was a natural horsewoman. Strickland was known for her aggressiveness and ability to get the most out of her horse.

Professional Women's Rodeo Association (PWRA) division sanctions all rodeo events for women—from breakaway and calf roping to bull riding. Women also participate in the PRCA, just as men do. Women in rodeo have worked hard to be taken seriously in the sport and to increase the prize money to equal that of men's.

JUNIOR RODEOS

Many professional cowboys and cowgirls today started their careers as members of the National Little Britches Rodeo Association (NLBRA). Created in 1952, the NLBRA currently has more than 1,500 kids competing in rodeos all over the country. It promotes 175 rodeos in thirty states. The NLBRA does not award cash prizes at its rodeos, but young people can win college scholarships, saddles, buckles,

John Shelton dismounts his horse after roping a calf. This high school athlete was competing at the Iowa High School Rodeo being held in Fort Madison, Iowa, on June 18, 2004. As a member of the Iowa High School Rodeo Association, Shelton loves meeting new people while participating in the sport he considers the greatest in the world.

and gift certificates. There are five divisions: little wranglers (ages 5 through 7), junior girls (ages 8 through 13), junior boys (ages 8–13), senior girls (ages 14 through 18), and senior boys (ages 14 through 18). Calf roping is promoted with junior versions of the sport called breakaway calf roping and goat tying. These events require less strength, but a young person still needs to have roping and horse-riding skills.

High school students can join the National High School Rodeo Association (NHSRA). The first NHSRA finals were held in 1949 in Hallettsville, Texas. Today, it has 12,500 members. Students can earn college scholarships, but to join they must have passing grades and be in good standing with their schools.

CALF ROPING IN ACTION

If you are a spectator at a rodeo, the first thing you notice is the smell of cattle and dirt in the air. The arena floor is made of soil turned up by a tractor so the ground is soft. The announcer shouts that the calf-roping event is next. You see the cowboy or cowgirl backing his or her horse into the corner of the three-sided, fenced box, waiting to run at top speed. The calf is next to the box in the chute. The barrier rope is looped around the calf's neck and stretches across the box. You wait with anticipation!

Before the rodeo started, a random drawing determined the order in which the calf ropers will be competing. The number of ropers participating varies from competition to competition. Yet whoever wins the event walks away with the purse—the combined entry fees of all the participants. The scoreline for the event has also been predetermined. The scoreline varies depending on the size of the particular arena in which the rodeo is being held.

THE ACTION-PACKED RUN

The announcer makes the call, and the gate is opened for the calf. The calf runs out of the chute past the scoreline that is marked in the dirt. Reaching this point releases the barrier rope across the box for the roper. If the roper were to break the barrier before the calf reaches this point, he would receive a ten-second penalty. This also ensures that all ropers begin the competition from the same point.

The broken barrier rope dangles at the front of the box *(far right, background)* as this cowboy aims his lariat just ahead of the calf he pursues. He hopes the rope will catch the calf perfectly. The eyelet can be seen at the back of the loop, midway down the length of the lariat. The other end of the rope is threaded through this to form a loop.

The roper has one rope in his mouth and swings another in a circle with his hand. The second rope is attached at one end to the saddle horn. The horse runs up behind the calf as the roper swings the rope over its head and around its neck. The horse has been trained to come to a stop once this has been achieved. Next, the roper gets off his horse and the horse backs up to bring the rope tight to keep the calf from going anywhere.

The roper runs over and grabs the calf from the flanks and throws it on its side. This is known as flanking. If the calf is already lying on the ground, the roper must pick the calf up and lay it down again. He ties the calf with the pigging string that he has been carrying in his mouth by grabbing one of the front legs and tying it with the two hind legs. Once the calf is securely tied, the roper throws his hands in the air, signaling the field judge to call time. At this point, the roper has completed his run. A great run is in nine seconds or less.

The roper remounts the horse and walks the horse forward a few steps to give the rope some slack. The calf at the end of the slacked rope must remain tied for six seconds. The roper waits while the tie is timed, hoping the calf doesn't break free before those six seconds are up!

JUDGING CALF ROPING

A calf roper must abide by specific rules to get a score. There are at least two judges who look for these in a calf-roping event: the starter judge and the field (or flag)

This calf is being taken to the ground by Chris Wooten at the National High School Finals Rodeo in Farmington, New Mexico, on July 22, 2002. Wooten has grabbed the calf's flank (the side of the calf between the ribs and hips) with his right hand and he is just releasing the calf's front leg.

judge. The starter judge stands next to the box. This judge starts the clock once the barrier is broken and the rider has left the box, also making sure the barrier is not broken too early. The rider will be disqualified if he leaves before the calf has crossed the scoreline in the arena. Once the roper goes after the calf, he or she must reach it within thirty-five seconds to avoid receiving "no time."

The field judge is positioned farther down the arena. Once the rider catches the calf and dismounts, this judge's role comes into play. He or she watches closely to make sure the tie is done correctly. If the string is wrapped around any three legs at least once and secured with a half hitch, it is a fair tie. The judge then makes sure the fair tie keeps the calf down for at least six seconds, timing this with a stopwatch. If the calf kicks free before this, the roper will receive "no time."

Brent Lewis signals to the judges that he has completed the tie during the National Finals Rodeo held in Las Vegas, Nevada, in 2000. The calf's front legs and one hind leg have been tied. The rope leading back to the horse is pulled taut.

If the judge sees the roper untie the calf after he has lifted his arms, he is immediately disqualified because the judge has not been allowed to time the tie.

AN IMPORTANT PARTNERSHIP

The roper must indeed be an athlete to succeed in calf roping, possessing such skills as speed and accuracy. However, his or her reliable and properly trained quarter horse is probably even more crucial to the outcome. This horse must be able to wait for its cue to leave the box, then take off at its top speed. The horse must be trained to stop once the catch has been made and be able to back up just enough to keep the lariat tight but not too tight as to drag the calf while its partner does his work. Dragging the calf can result in being disqualified, paying up to a $100 fine (if paid at the event, this is added to the purse) and receiving "no time."

THE CALVES IN COMPETITION

The calves used in PRCA competitions weigh between 220 to 280 pounds (100 to 127 kilograms). Most calves used in professional competitions are of a breed native to North America—such as Texas Longhorn—or Brahman, or a breed that is a cross between the two. These calves are roped only about thirty times before they grow too big for the event.

Just as with the order of participants, the calf is picked at random. Some ropers claim they can tell a calf's personality by checking out the calf before the event.

Timed Events Vs. Roughstock Events

The roughstock events of rodeo (bull, bareback, and bronc riding) are judged on technique, and therefore the judge's calls are subjective. Calf roping, on the other hand, is a timed event where the contestant is racing the clock and the time of his fellow contestants. Team roping and barrel racing are also timed events.

Yet the only predictable thing is that once released from the chute, the calf will run. Some may be faster or slower than others. If the calf has made the run before, it will usually remember where the exit of the arena is and take off toward it.

COMPETITIONS FOR KIDS

Young people can compete in competitions very similar to the calf-roping event for adults, but these events require less strength. If you want to start competing with others in your age group, consider the following options.

Breakaway Calf Roping

This event is just like calf roping, except you don't actually have to get off your horse to tie the calf. Once the competition begins (by breaking the barrier once the calf has crossed the scoreline), you pursue the calf and throw the lariat over the calf's head where it catches around its neck. At the same time, you bring your horse to a stop. The calf will continue to run, which will cause the lariat to break away from the saddle horn where it is attached by a string. The end of the lariat

Champion ropers, like other great athletes, have good days and bad days. Here, ReAnn Zancanella reacts after her lariat misses the calf. Zancanella, of Southeastern Oklahoma State, was competing in the breakaway roping event at the College National Finals Rodeo in Casper, Wyoming, on June 17, 2005.

attached to the saddle horn has a white flag on the end of it. The white flag makes it possible for the judge to tell when the rope has been released from the horse. The judge times how long it takes for you to reach the calf to the point the rope breaks free from the saddle horn.

Goat Tying

In the goat-tying event, you will ride your horse to a goat tied to a stake in the ground about fifty yards (forty-six meters) from the starting line. Once you have reached the goat, you must get off your horse, run over to the goat, and throw the goat to the ground. You then tie three legs of the goat together with your pigging string.

A young cowgirl competes in the goat-tail tying competition at Li'l Buckaroo Rodeo in Pinedale, Wyoming, in July 2005. The judge makes her way over to make sure the tie around the goat's tail remains tied for at least five seconds.

The goat must stay tied for at least five seconds, and if you allow your horse to touch the goat or the rope during the event, you will be disqualified.

Goat-Tail Tying

This event is different in that you ride your horse over to a hitching post, jump off, and run over to a goat that is staked to the ground by a rope. You then tie a ribbon around the goat's tail. The ribbon must stay on for at least five seconds, and the horse must stay hitched the entire time. This event is geared toward competitors aged five to eight.

GREAT CALF ROPERS OF THE WORLD

CHAPTER 3

There have been many great champions in calf roping. The amount of money won in a season by a calf roper determines his or her placement in the world championships. That is why calf ropers will travel and compete all over the country. In 1989, one calf roper missed qualifying for the Wrangler National Finals Rodeo (NFR) by a little over one dollar. The most money to be won in calf roping in a single year was won by Cody Ohl. He won $222,794 in 1998.

CHAMPION MALE CALF ROPERS

The beginning of professional calf roping started in 1929 when Everett Bowman won the first calf-roping championship. Bowman later won two more championships in 1935 and 1937.

Toots Mansfield won the world championship for calf roping seven times between the years 1939 and 1950. Mansfield began roping on his uncle's ranch in Texas just after finishing high school. He started roping to earn money for groceries during the Great Depression. Over the years, he earned much more than grocery money. Mansfield was considered one of the best ropers of all time. He would practice roping anything he could find. His passion for the sport of rodeo and calf roping led him to serve as the president of the PRCA for four years and to start his own school for young ropers in the 1950s.

Roy Cooper, pictured here, is considered one of the greatest calf ropers in history. Not only has Cooper won every major rodeo in the United States, in 2000 he became the first cowboy to pass the $2 million mark in career earnings. He also excels at team roping and steer roping.

The man with the most world titles in calf roping is Dean Oliver. He won eight world championships from 1955 to 1969 and three world all-around titles (awarded to the athlete who wins the most money in two or more events) in a row from 1963 to 1965. Dean Oliver is one of the few calf ropers who started as an adult. Oliver first saw a calf-roping competition in Idaho. He was astonished to learn that a man could win $300 in only a few seconds just for tying down a calf with some rope. He decided he wanted that kind of "easy" money and started practicing roping. His family made huge sacrifices for him to become one of the greatest calf ropers of all times. According to one story, Oliver once spent his last

World champion Cody Ohl from Stephenville, Texas, flanks a calf during a rodeo in April 2005. Ohl tore three tendons in his right knee at the 2001 Wrangler National Finals Rodeo in Las Vegas, Nevada, but still won all-around champion and world champion tie-down. After making a comeback to win the 2003 world champion tie-down, Ohl told ESPN.com, "This one is so special. This was like coming back from a handicap . . ."

dollars on a horse instead of food for his family. In the long run, however, his family benefited greatly from his winnings. He is still involved in the world of calf roping as a journalist, writing articles about current competitions and ropers in *Western Horseman*.

Roy Cooper is one of the few men to have won three world titles in one season. In 1983, he won world all-around champion cowboy, world champion calf roper, and champion steer roper. Indeed, Roy Cooper has earned his nickname of Super Looper. He won world championship titles in calf roping five years in a row, from 1980 to 1984. It seems that calf roping was in Cooper's blood. His mother was an all-around and calf-roping champion. Both his father and mother taught their boys the art of calf roping on their ranch. He began competing in rodeos at ten years of age. Cooper suffered from asthma as a child, and it was not certain that he could compete professionally. However, he continued to practice every day after school and eventually overcame this obstacle. Cooper had become a great roper by the time he reached high school, winning the 1973 NHSRA championship and scholarships to numerous colleges. When he graduated from college, Cooper joined the professional circuit. Overall, Cooper has won eight world titles, six in tie-down roping. In 1979, Cooper suffered from a hand injury while he was practicing. This injury required him to have metal pins placed in his hands. However, he still went to the NFR and won. He is married to the daughter of a professional calf roper and has settled down in Decatur, Texas, where he and his wife own a restaurant. Cooper has written a book on calf roping, used today by many who are learning the sport.

Fred Whitfield and Cody Ohl, two Texans who also happen to be friends, are currently considered the best in the sport of calf roping. Whitfield has won six world championships since 1991. He has been roping since he was six years old. He learned from a friend who was the son of an oilman for whom his mother worked. Whitfield competed in his first rodeo at the age of nine at the National Little Britches Rodeo. Whitfield was very driven. Growing up, he would rope about 200 calves a day after school. Whitfield is the fourth African American to be inducted in the National Cowboy Hall of Fame, located in Oklahoma, and the first to win a world championship in calf roping.

Cody Ohl has won four world championships since 1997. In 2003, Ohl set a world record with the fasted run at 6.5 seconds. Ohl has the same resolve that so many of these cowboys possess. He hurt his knee in the 2001 Wrangler National Finals and had to have three knee surgeries and many hours of rehabilitation. But this did not stop Ohl. In 2003, he won the world all-around championship and the world tie-down roping title. Ohl had not been sure that he would ever succeed again as a champion calf roper, which made winning the title that year even more rewarding.

CHAMPION FEMALE CALF ROPERS

Lucille Mulhall is one of the first notable ropers in rodeo history. She won a bet against President Theodore Roosevelt when she successfully roped a coyote. One woman who competed in calf roping when there were few competitions for women was Jewel Frost Duncan. She was the first woman to compete in the West of the Pecos rodeo in 1929. Duncan was good friends with Isora DeRacy Young, who also competed in calf-roping events. The two of them often traveled to competitions together as the only cowgirls to challenge cowboys in roping.

Sue Pirtle is considered one of rodeo's most versatile cowgirls. Pirtle has won eleven GRA world titles including all-around cowgirl and champion bareback rider. Pirtle started in calf roping in her hometown of Stonewall, Oklahoma, when she was eleven years old. She used to watch the men at a nearby ranch practice their rodeo skills, and over time they began showing her how to ride and rope. When Pirtle was competing in calf-roping tournaments full-time, she practiced her roping skills about ten hours a week. She traveled from rodeo to rodeo during the 1970s, enjoying the excitement of going to new towns, but over the years she got tired of being away from home. She quit the rodeo in her thirties. A TV movie, *Rodeo Girl*, was made about her life in 1980. She appeared in it, doing most of the stunts herself. Today, Sue designs art deco furniture. Her son, Ty Hays, continues the tradition of calf roping and has been to the NFR.

The first major title Kim Williamson won was the 1984 National High School Rodeo Finalist for barrel racing. Here, she is seen during the event that would lead to one of her most recent titles—breakaway calf roping world champion. Besides being a champion calf roper, Williamson is the first woman to ever win dual team roping world titles: she won as heeler in 2000 and as header in 2003.

Kim Williamson was the 2004 all-around world champion at the WPRA All Women's Rodeo. She has been a finalist and champion in many breakaway-roping and calf-roping events. Williamson started learning how to ride and rope when she was eight years old, and she roped her first calf when she was ten. Her father taught her many of the calf-roping skills she uses today. Of women calf ropers, she considers Sue Pirtle; Betty Gayle Cooper, the beloved champion, coach, and instructor of the sport; and Gina Brooks to be some of the best women ropers around. Gina Brooks has won seven titles in calf roping. She and Williamson often traveled together on the rodeo circuit.

GET TO KNOW A CHAMPION

The National Little Britches Rodeo Association includes profiles of several of its World Champions on its Web site. Here is a brief biography of Tyler Schnaufer, the 2004 NLBRA world champion junior breakaway roper.

Age:	14
Hometown:	Pueblo, Colorado
Favorite Movie:	*Napoleon Dynamite*
Rodeo Hero:	Rich Skelton
Favorite Food:	Prime rib
Hobbies:	Hunting

You can learn about other NLBRA champions by visiting http://www.nlbra.com/2004_World_Champions.htm.

JUNIOR CALF ROPERS

The National Little Britches Rodeo Association sanctions rodeos for kids ages five through eighteen. The NLBRA has three age divisions: little wranglers, ages five to seven; juniors, ages eight to thirteen; and seniors, ages fourteen to eighteen. The little wranglers are too young to rope a calf, so they compete in goat tail–untying. Junior boys and girls and senior girls compete in breakaway roping and goat tying. The senior boys are the only division that competes in calf roping.

All calf-roping champions, whether men, women, or young people, have a few things in common. They love the rodeo and are driven to succeed in one of the oldest sports. Some of these champions have been competing since they were six years old, and others, like Dean Oliver, started as adults. Their stories show that age doesn't matter if you have skills, determination, and a place to practice your craft.

GETTING STARTED IN CALF ROPING

Now you have learned a little bit of the history of rodeo and calf roping. You have gotten to know some champions and are aware of the training and determination this sport calls for. Do you think you have what it takes to be a champion calf roper? If so, there is a very important partner and equipment you will need in order to become a rodeo cowboy or rodeo cowgirl. Remember, many cowboys and cowgirls have not grown up on farms or ranches but learn these skills through workshops and classes.

EVERY ASPIRING CALF ROPER NEEDS A HORSE

The very first thing you need for calf roping is a horse. Then, you need to know how to ride it. Calf-roping champion Kim Williamson holds training clinics in roping at her ranch in Queen Creek, Arizona. She encourages young people to learn how to care for horses. Like people, horses have personalities. If a horse is treated well as a youngster, it will turn out to be a good horse. Indeed, your horse is your greatest ally. Your horse is supposed to know its job in the calf-roping event. A properly trained quarter horse has the ability to wait in the box until the time is right and then take off at full speed behind the calf. Your horse will act entirely by itself by digging its hind legs into the ground once you have stopped and then back up just enough to tighten the rope that has been thrown around the calf's head and is attached to the saddle horn. Fred

Whitfield claims the majority of his wins were due to his well-trained horses. The horse does 80 percent of the work while the rider carries out the last 20 percent.

According to Roy Cooper in *Calf Roping*, when you go to buy a horse that has been trained for roping, you want the trainer to get on it and show you that the horse is capable of the job. You should also find out how the horse was trained and with what equipment to make sure you are able to do the same. Also, if you only ride your horse at rodeo time, your horse will get bored and stop working for you. You need to add a little variety to the horse's life with different types of

As we have learned, the sport of calf roping derives from the real-life practices of cowhands. Here, we see a cowboy's well-trained horse pulling the rope taut as his rider administers medication to a calf's eyes during a cattle drive in Colorado.

rides: ride fast, ride slow, ride one day over hills, the next day over pastures, rope on your horse one day, take it for a long trot the next. Horses need days off, too, just like you do. On those days, allow your horse to relax just like you plan to do! When you are ready to rope, be sure to warm your horse up by riding different loping, or easy gait, circles. Your horse will be more relaxed and responsive.

GEAR FOR YOUR HORSE

Roping saddles vary. You should consult with a saddle maker or seller, or a knowledgeable roper for advice on which saddle is right for you. Your roping saddle should be padded and fit close to the horse's back. Your stirrups should be wider than most stirrups so you can get on and off your horse really fast. The bit that fits into the horse's mouth must be chosen depending on the type

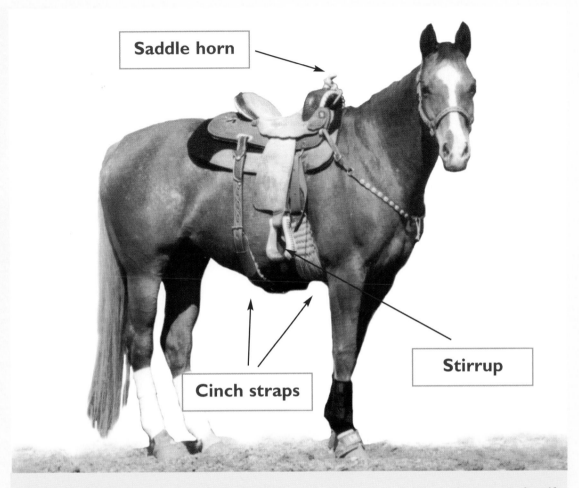

Saddle horn

Cinch straps

Stirrup

The type of saddle a cowboy or cowgirl has depends on his or her rodeo event. A calf roper's saddle is smaller at the back end and is low in the front. This helps a roper leave the saddle quickly. Also, a smaller saddle horn gives a roper's horse better leverage to help hold the cow at the other end. Cinch straps are fastened around the horse's flanks to hold the saddle in place. Stirrups are placed to fall at just the right angle for the rider's boot.

of horse you have. You don't want to put a severe bit in the horse's mouth if he doesn't need it. The bit is attached to the chin strap and reins. The reins are what you will use to control the direction of your horse. You will have a pulley or large ring attached to the saddle swell. The jerk line is a rope that goes from the horse's mouth or bit through the rings and is tucked into your belt. When you get off your horse, this will pull the line just enough to get the horse to hold its position. As you run over to your calf, the last bit of rope should pull out of your belt leaving the right amount of tension on the line.

THE ROPES YOU WILL NEED

You will need two types of rope. One rope should be 25 to 26 feet long (7 to 8 m) and made of nylon. Ropes come in different weights and strengths. Beginners are encouraged to use a rope labeled 9.5 or 10.0 millimeters. These ropes are lighter and softer. Your ropes should be "poly ropes" made of polyethylene, so they won't be too stiff and won't break easily. The second type of rope you need is a pigging string. You will want at least two pigging strings, one to carry in your mouth and the other

A cowboy races to tie three of a calf's legs with his pigging string during a calf-roping event in Anchorage, Alaska. The traditional tie with the pigging string is two wraps and a hooey—the final wrap that is a half-hitch tie.

to tuck in your belt in case you lose the first one in the middle of a competition. You probably want to take care of these as you don't want to end up with a mouth full of dirt. These ropes are usually about 6 feet (1.83 m) long and are used to rope the calf's legs. They come in different levels of stiffness. A stiff pigging string is harder to handle but keeps the calf in place longer. Beginners should practice with a softer rope. They are easier to handle and are less likely to hurt your hands.

Kim Williamson instructs a young roper who has just successfully roped a dummy calf. Williamson offers clinics on weekends and after school hours, as well as private lessons all throughout the year. One tip she gives to young riders is to practice their swing of the rope to such a point that their last will be as good as their first.

THE DUMMY CALF

The best way to start practicing roping is with a pretend calf. Many ropers suggest practicing your roping ability on a bucket filled with feed and then practicing on a dummy. A typical dummy is a bale of hay with a fake calf head, usually made of wood, sticking out of one end. Cooper suggests standing six steps behind your target looping your rope. You want to run a few steps and then throw. Your view of the

Protecting Livestock

Some organizations such as People for the Ethical Treatment of Animals (PETA) have been fighting hard to have calf roping banned from rodeos. They are concerned that some calves get hurt when they are roped around their necks. The PRCA recognizes the need for strict rules in handling cattle and horses. Rules and regulations protect horses and calves from being mistreated in competition and training. During a competition, judges will disqualify contestants if they see them being too rough with the livestock. There are more than sixty rules and regulations in place to protect animals used in the rodeo.

dummy is the back of its head. You should try to have a little dip in the loop. The dip causes the rope to curl up so that when you throw it around the calf's neck it will flip up over its head. As you run toward the dummy, keep the throw smooth and at the same speed. Once the rope hits, you will pull on it and tighten the slack.

ABOUT THE CALVES

You will want to practice on real calves before you go to competitions. Catching a running calf is a little trickier than roping a dummy. There are certain rules you must follow in handling a calf because you can really hurt it if you aren't careful. When you rope the calf, you want to make sure that the rope around its neck has enough slack so the calf can breathe. Flanking the calf means taking the calf and holding it under the belly or flanks as you grab its right front leg. One arm is over the calf's back while the other grabs the leg to keep the calf from running off. You must lift the calf clearly off the ground and on its side. Once you have the calf on its side, you will then use the pigging string you have carried in your mouth to tie three legs together. Most ropers tie one of the front legs first and then grab a hold

Most of the skills and artistry of calf roping have been passed down from generation to generation, having first been mastered by the vaqueros in Spanish America. It is an exhilarating sport for both spectator and participant. Cowboys and cowgirls race against the clock and each other, and must have trust in their horse and all they have learned from hours and hours of practice in order to succeed.

of the two hind legs and rope all together. If you are just beginning, you can enter contests through the National Little Britches Association that don't require you to actually lift a calf. For instance, breakaway roping just requires you to get the rope around the calf's head. Other events, such as goat tying, require you to lift a goat and tie its legs; however, a goat weighs much less than a calf.

CONCLUSION

Now you know the basics of calf roping and what it takes to get started. You may have what it takes to one day become a professional calf roper. To find out more about opportunities you have in your state, go to the Web site for the National Little Britches Association. (See For More Information on page 42.) This Web site will allow you to look up your state and find the rodeos nearest you and where you can get training. This exciting sport offers so many opportunities, from college scholarships to prize money. Once you get the equipment and begin to learn the skills, all you need is time and commitment to practicing to become the best calf roper you can be!

List of Champions

The PRCA, first known as the Cowboys Turtle Association, then as the Rodeo Cowboys Association, is the oldest and largest rodeo organization. The PRCA paved the way for many of the governing bodies of rodeo that exist today. Each of these organizations celebrates its own world champions. Below is a list of PRCA world champions and rodeo records.

NAME	CHAMPION'S RESIDENCE	WINNING YEARS
Everett Bowman	Hillside, Arizona	1929
Jake McClure	Lovington, New Mexico	1930
Herb Meyers	Okmulgee, Oklahoma	1931
Richard Merchant	Kirkland, Arizona	1932
Bill McFarlane	Red Bluff, California	1933
Irby Mundy	Shamrock, Texas	1934
Everett Bowman	Hillside, Arizona	1935
Clyde Burk	Comanche, Oklahoma	1936
Everett Bowman	Hillside, Arizona	1937
Clyde Burk	Comanche, Oklahoma	1938
Toots Mansfield	Bandera, Texas	1939–1941
Clyde Burk	Comanche, Oklahoma	1942
Toots Mansfield	Bandera, Texas	1943
Clyde Burk	Comanche, Oklahoma	1944
Toots Mansfield	Bandera, Texas	1945
Royce Sewalt	King, Texas	1946
Troy Fort	Lovington, New Mexico	1947
Toots Mansfield	Bandera, Texas	1948
Troy Fort	Lovington, New Mexico	1949
Toots Mansfield	Bandera, Texas	1950
Don McLaughlin	Fort Worth, Texas	1951–1954

NAME	CHAMPION'S RESIDENCE	WINNING YEARS
Dean Oliver	Boise, Idaho	1955
Ray Wharton	Bandera, Texas	1956
Don McLaughlin	Fort Worth, Texas	1957
Dean Oliver	Boise, Idaho	1958
Jim Bob Altizer	Del Rio, Texas	1959
Dean Oliver	Boise, Idaho	1960–1964
Glen Franklin	House, New Mexico	1965
Junior Garrison	Marlow, Oklahoma	1966
Glen Franklin	House, New Mexico	1967
Glen Franklin	House, New Mexico	1968
Dean Oliver	Boise, Idaho	1969
Junior Garrison	Marlow, Oklahoma	1970
Phil Lyne	George West, Texas	1971
Phil Lyne	George West, Texas	1972
Ernie Taylor	Hugo, Oklahoma	1973
Tom Ferguson	Miami, Oklahoma	1974
Jeff Copenhaver	Spokane, Washington	1975
Roy Cooper	Durant, Oklahoma	1976
Jim Gladstone	Cardston, Alberta	1977
Dave Brock	Pueblo, Colorado	1978
Paul Tierney	Rapid City, South Dakota	1979
Roy Cooper	Durant, Oklahoma	1980–1984
Joe Beaver	Victoria, Texas	1985
Chris Lybbert	Argyle, Texas	1986
Joe Beaver	Victoria, Texas	1987
Joe Beaver	Victoria, Texas	1988
Rabe Rabon	San Antonio, Florida	1989

NAME	CHAMPION'S RESIDENCE	WINNING YEAR
Troy Pruitt	Lennox, South Dakota	1990
Fred Whitfield	Cypress, Texas	1991
Joe Beaver	Huntsville, Texas	1992
Joe Beaver	Huntsville, Texas	1993
Herbert Theriot	Wiggins, Mississippi	1994
Fred Whitfield	Hockley, Texas	1995
Fred Whitfield	Hockley, Texas	1996
Cody Ohl	Orchard, Texas	1997
Cody Ohl	Orchard, Texas	1998
Fred Whitfield	Hockley, Texas	1999
Fred Whitfield	Hockley, Texas	2000
Cody Ohl	Stephenville, Texas	2001
Fred Whitfield	Hockley, Texas	2002
Cody Ohl	Stephenville, Texas	2003
Monty Lewis	Hereford, Texas	2004

Most Money Won in a Regular Season (prior to NFR)
$152,670, Cody Ohl, 2001

Most Money Won in One Year
$222,794, Cody Ohl, 1998

Fastest Times in Calf Roping
(Area conditions, sizes, and scorelines vary.)

5.7 Seconds—Lee Phillips in Assiniboia, Saskatchewan, 1978

6.5 Seconds—Cody Ohl at Wrangler NFR, 2003
Clint Robinson at Amarillo, Texas, 2004

6.7 Seconds—Joe Beaver in West Jordan, Utah, 1986
Stran Smith in Dallas, Texas, 2001
Cody Ohl in Dallas, Texas, 2001

Glossary

barrier rope The rope stretched across the opening of the box during the calf-roping event. The calf roper must pass the rope before the event begins.

box The area from which the calf roper starts. The barrier rope stretches across the opening of the box.

breaking the barrier A term used when the calf roper leaves the box and breaks the barrier rope.

chute The area in which the calf waits before the calf-roping event begins. This narrow area has a gate at the front of it that opens into the arena.

cow town A town or city that is based on a cattle market or is a shipping center for cattle.

curl The upward bend of the rope as it loops over the calf's head. A visible curl indicates the rope has been thrown well.

dummy A bale of hay with a fake calf head sticking out of one end. The dummy is used in practicing calf roping.

flanking A term used to describe the procedure of grabbing the calf's leg with one hand and its underbelly with the other hand and then flipping the calf.

Great Depression A period of time marked by unemployment and low economic activity that began with the stock market crash of 1929 and lasted until 1939.

half hitch A simple knot that is tied by passing one end of the rope around the three legs of the calf and back across the main part of the rope, then through the resulting loop.

lariat A lasso with a noose for catching livestock.

no score What the judge states when the calf roper does not get a score for the event. This occurs when the calf roper breaks regulations during the event or is unable to rope the calf.

Old West A term used to refer to the way of life in the western part of North America beyond the settled frontier, particularly between the years of 1860 and 1900.

open range Unfenced land for livestock grazing.

pigging string The string used to tie three legs of the calf together. It is smaller than the rope used around the neck of the calf.

quarter horse A breed of horse that is especially capable of running short distances quickly, such as a quarter mile, from which it gets its name.

rodeo A contest of professional athletes competing for money in organized events involving horses and cattle.

run The entire process from the moment the calf roper leaves the box until the calf is roped and the contestant lifts up his or her hands.

saddle horn A piece of the saddle that sticks up out of the seat and is used to hold one end of the rope during calf roping.

sanctioned Validated or given approval in official procedures.

score The distance between the chute opening and the scoreline.

scoreline The line the calf crosses in the arena before the calf roper can break the barrier to start the event.

For More Information

American Junior Rodeo Association
4501 Armstrong Street
San Angelo, TX 76903
(352) 658-8009

National High School Rodeo Association
12001 Tejon Street, Suite 128
Denver, CO 80234
(303) 452-0820
Web site: http://www.nhsra.org

National Little Britches Rodeo Association
1045 W. Rio Grande Street
Colorado Springs, CO 80906
(800) 763-3694
Web site: http://www.nlbra.org

Professional Rodeo Cowboys Association
101 ProRodeo Drive
Colorado Springs, CO 80919
(719) 528-4761
Web site: http://www.prorodeo.org

United States Calf Ropers Association
P.O. Box 690
Giddings, TX 78942
(979) 542-1239
Web site: http://uscra.com

Women's Professional Rodeo Association
235 Lake Plaza Drive, Suite 134
Colorado Springs, CO 80906
(719) 576-0900
Web site: http://www.wpra.com

WEB SITES

Due to the changing nature of Internet links, the Rosen Publishing Group, Inc., has developed an online list of Web sites related to the subject of this book. This site is updated regularly. Please use this link to access the list:

http://www.rosenlinks.com/woro/caro

For Further Reading

Byers, Chester. *Roping: Trick and Fancy Rope Spinning*. Bedford, MA: Applewood Books, 1988.

Campion, Lynn. *Rodeo*. Guilford, CT: The Lyons Press, 2002.

Cooper, Roy. *Calf Roping*. Colorado Springs, CO: Western Horseman, 1984.

Sherman, Joseph. *Welcome to the Rodeo*. Chicago, IL: Heinemann Library, 2000.

Tinkelman, Murray. *Little Britches Rodeo*. New York, NY: Greenwillow Books, 1985.

Bibliography

Allen, Mike. "Ellensburg Rodeo Hall of Fame." August 24, 2004. Retrieved March 1, 2005 (http://www.kvnews.com/articles/2004/08/24/news/news03.prt).

Campion, Lynn. *Rodeo*. Guilford, CT: The Lyons Press, 2002.

Cooper, Roy. *Calf Roping*. Colorado Springs, CO: Western Horseman, 1984.

Lawrence and Associates. *The National Cowgirl Museum and Hall of Fame 2004 Yearbook*. Fort Worth, TX: National Cowgirl Museum and Hall of Fame, 2004.

Morthland, John. "Spurred On." *Texas Monthly*, December 2000, pp. 98–102.

National High School Rodeo Association. "About Us." Retrieved March 1, 2005 (http://www.nhsra.org/about_faq.html).

National Little Britches Rodeo Association. "Meet Your 2004 World Champions." Retrieved March 1, 2005 (http://nlbra.com/archives/2004%20World%20champs/Tyler_Schnaufer.htm).

Oliver, Dean, and Jimmie Hurley. "The Best Calf Roper." *Western Horseman*. Retrieved March 1, 2005 (http://westernhorseman.com/stories/02042005/rod_2004112000l.shtml).

Professional Rodeo and Cowboy Association. "ProRodeo World Records." Retrieved March 1, 2005 (http://sports.espn.go.com/prorodeo/news/story?page=g_WorldRec_2003).

Sherman, Joseph. *Welcome to the Rodeo*. Chicago, IL: Heinemann Library, 2000.

Tinkelman, Murray. *Little Britches Rodeo*. New York, NY: Greenwillow Books, 1985.

United States Calf Ropers Association. Retrieved March 1, 2005 (http://uscra.com/rules.asp).

Whitfield, Fred. "Biography." Retrieved March 1, 2005 (http://www.fredwhitfield.com/biography/).

Williamson, Kim. "The Official Website of Kim Williamson." Retrieved March 1, 2005 (http://www.kimwilliamson.net/biography.htm).

Women's Professional Rodeo Association. "Women's Rodeo History." Retrieved March 1, 2005 (http://www.wpra.com/rodeohistory.htm).

Calf Roping

Wooden, Wayne, and Gavin Ehringer. *Rodeo in America: Wranglers, Roughstock, and Paydirt.* Lawrence, KS: University Press of Kansas, 1996.

World of Rodeo. "Dean Oliver." Retrieved March 1, 2005 (http://www.worldofrodeo.com/stories/prcahalloffame.htm).

World of Rodeo. "Roy Cooper." Retrieved March 1, 2005 (http://www.worldofrodeo.com/stories/prcahalloffame.htm).

Index

B

Bowman, Everett, 10, 20
breakaway calf roping, 11, 12, 17–18
Brooks, Gina, 25
bulldogging, 8
bull riding, 11, 17

C

calf roping
   calves for, 16–17, 33–35
   gear and ropes for, 29–32
   horses for, 28–29
   judging of, 15–16
   practicing, 32–33
   run, description of, 13–15
cattle drive, 6–7
Cody, William F. "Buffalo Bill," 8–9
Cooper, Betty Gayle, 25
Cooper, Roy "Super Looper," 23, 29, 32
Cowboy Turtles Association, 10

D

Duncan, Jewel Frost, 24

G

goat-tail tying, 19
goat tying, 12, 18–19

H

Hays, Ty, 24

M

Mansfield, Toots, 20
Mulhall, Lucille, 24

N

National Cowboy Hall of Fame, 24
National Finals Rodeo (NFR), 23
National High School Rodeo Association
   (NHSRA), 12, 23
National Little Britches Rodeo Association
   (NLBRA), 11–12, 26, 35

O

Oakley, Annie, 9
Ohl, Cody, 20, 23, 24
Oliver, Dean, 21–23, 27

P

People for the Ethical Treatment of Animals
   (PETA), 33
Pickett, Bill, 8
Pirtle, Sue, 24, 25
Pony Express, 8
prizes/awards/purses, 10, 11, 13, 16, 20, 21,
   23, 35
Professional Rodeo Cowboys Association
   (PRCA), 10, 11, 16, 20, 33

R

rodeo
   history of, 6–12, 28
   women in, 10–11, 24–25
Rodeo Association of America (RAA), 9–10
Rodeo Cowboys Association, 10

S

Strickland, Mabel, 10

Calf Roping

W

Western Horseman magazine, 23
Whitfield, Fred, 23–24, 28–29
Wild West shows, 8, 9, 10
Williamson, Kim, 25, 28

Women's Professional Rodeo Association
    (WPRA), 10–11, 25
Wrangler ProRodeo Tours, 10

Y

Young, Isora DeRacy, 24

ABOUT THE AUTHOR

Kimberly King has her Ph.D. in counseling and teaches others how to respect and treat children to help them grow up to be great cowboys and cowgirls. She lives with her husband in Richardson, Texas. She attends rodeos and has become a fan of the customs real cowboys and cowgirls have grown up with such as country music, big belt buckles, big trucks, and appreciating a good throw of a rope.

PHOTO CREDITS

Designer: Les Kanturek; **Editor**: Leigh Ann Cobb